MW00899096

John Wesley

CHURCH MOUSE

Evelyn Anne Johnson-Neal

ISBN 978-1-0980-3512-9 (paperback)
ISBN 978-1-0980-3513-6 (digital)

Copyright © 2021 by Evelyn Anne Johnson-Neal

All rights reserved. No part of this publication may be reproduced, distributed, or transmitted in any form or by any means, including photocopying, recording, or other electronic or mechanical methods without the prior written permission of the publisher. For permission requests, solicit the publisher via the address below.

Christian Faith Publishing, Inc.
832 Park Avenue
Meadville, PA 16335
www.christianfaithpublishing.com

Printed in the United States of America

John Wesley Church Mouse...
'Twas the day before Christmas
and all through the
church...
no one was talking. They
were all hard at work.
John Wesley Church Mouse was
concerned as he scurried about.
Checking on staff members, he
began running his route.

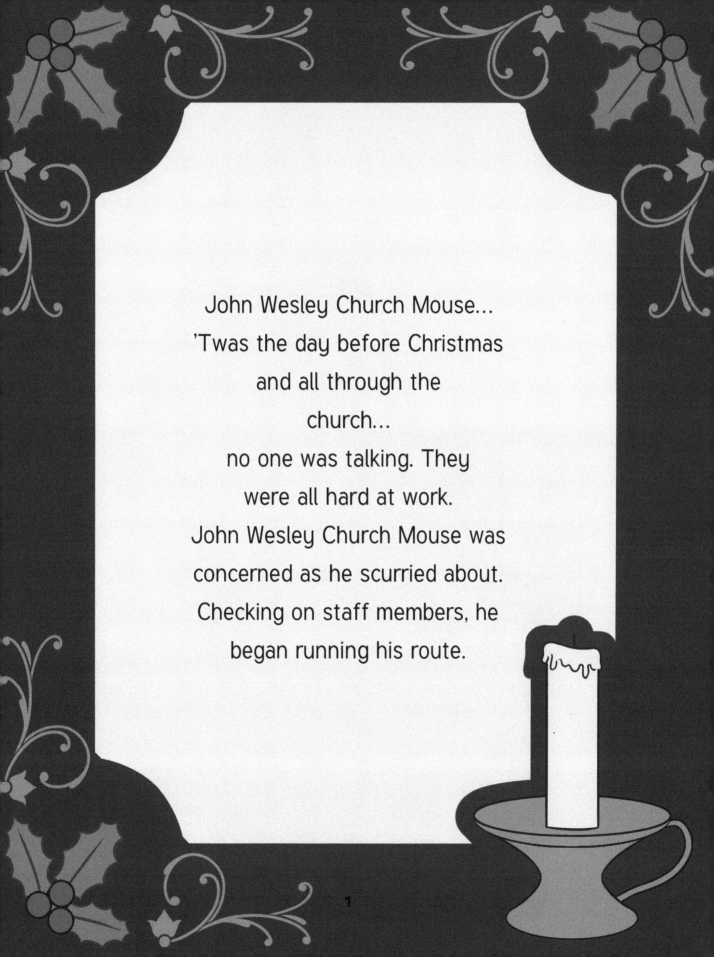

John Wesley comes from many generations of
church mice
who all had a mission to watch over
the staff of Chapin Church.
John Wesley's great-great-great
grandfather, John Wesley the First,
was the very first John Wesley Church Mouse
in the year 1889, to be completely precise!

His service to Chapin Church began in
the small church at Wessinger's Cross
Roads with only nineteen members!
The old man John Wesley Church Mouse
packed up his stuff after the fire in 1892
and hitched a ride in a box of hymnals.
Thus, he was transported to his new home...a
small wooden church in the city of Chapin.
After retiring, his son, John Wesley Church Mouse
Jr., was almost blown away by a terrible tornado
in 1936 that few folks today will remember!

The faithful forty, the church membership then,

rebuilt Chapin Church on Lexington Avenue.

It stands there today as Chapin Community Church.

In this Little Church, as we lovingly call it, John Wesley

Church Mouse III took care of the little brick church.

Reverend Albert Cox (1967) worked with John Wesley

for seventeen years to bring in many new members

whose souls Jesus the Christ would go on to win!

The faithful 40 soon became 151 members

in the year 1975.

Stepping out completely on faith and
with Gospel intentionality,
the small congregation moved across
Lexington Avenue to the present site...
(Can you imagine their immense faith
and tremendous foresight?)
when this small congregation, in a great leap
of faith, paid $8,000 for 9.8 acres and, along
with the now John Wesley Church Mouse IV,
built our Metal Church where today the youth
group and one contemporary service reside!

John Wesley IV took very good care of our
own Reverend Cox, his lovely wife Margie, and
their three children, while he also watched
over the church in a most careful way,
I must say!

10

Then came Reverend Bert Watson with his wife
and strongest supporter, Miss Lessie. His manner
was always distinguished and very encouraging!
John Wesley Church Mouse V kept Reverend
Watson's shoes brightly polished...
until young Reverend John Wesley Hipp
arrived at our church with his sweet wife
Carol, a teacher, and their two children...
but no relation to the church mouse, I'm sure!

Each minister and congregation laid down another stepping
stone, preparing us all for our church's mission today!
After building our new church sanctuary with
Reverend Jody Flowers, his precious wife, Michelle,
and their son, Andrew, in the year 2009, the faith
of our congregation was strengthened. And...
as each of our founding fathers, past congregations,
and all of our ministers had helped clear cut the way,
our church could look outward to the least, last, and lost...

Our mission... God's vision...
Obedience is what God demands!

But now back to the present and John
Wesley Church Mouse VI,
son to John Wesley Church Mouse V and grandson
to the Fourth, the Third, Junior, and the First!
Pastor Jody Flowers is the one for whom God was waiting…
as John Wesley Church Mouse VI
scampered onward…forthwith!

As I said, it is now Christmas Eve.
All through the church the hustle and bustle
were raising the level of anticipation.
John Wesley Church Mouse found Pastor Jody
hard at work on his Christmas Eve sermon
in his special office under the church.

14

God, through the Holy Spirit, was looking
over Pastor Jody's shoulder. So John
Wesley turned and tiptoed quietly out.

Back in the main office, those cute little elves,
Emily, Marcie, and Caroline,
giggle and grin as they hide some
staff gifts under the tree.
Faithful and dear, JW finds sweet Miss Alice, whom
even today is working away on year-end reports!
He hears a big chuckle from the office of Paul...all
families in need have received their Christmas cheer.

Paul smiles at Sharon, his patient wife and
Sunday school teacher, as they give the
Lord Jesus Christ a special high sign.
Satisfied that the main office is all on schedule,
John Wesley Church Mouse checks out one
last back office to be explicitly sure that
Rick is okay and his plans are all set.
John Wesley quietly retreats when he sees
Rick on his knees in prayer by his desk
on this inspiring eve of the Yule!
John Wesley Church Mouse VI is feeling the
pressure of completing his assignment on time!
Quickly scurrying and hurrying down the back hall.

"Hmmm, where is Curt? I am sure he's close by."
A last-minute light check or placing the
hand bells that later will sweetly chime!

Whew, this campus is huge for little mouse legs.
But John Wesley proceeds with his
mouse power full speed...
to check on the children's wing, but
preschool is out for the holiday season.

So the children's minister Miss Natalie, and the
nursery coordinator Andrea, and all of their crew
are at home preparing for the coming of Christmas
as they all hang up stockings high up on those
cute wooden pegs! In each home, the families
anticipate a most blessed Christmas morn!
John Wesley is tired but will not be daunted...
Just a few more of the staff left to see!

Uh-oh, this might be trouble, John Wesley

thinks as he takes off in a gallop...

down the back hall just to see what is

this unusual clatter. Everyone should be

gone. Is this hall now haunted?

Is it the Spirit of Christmas Past that

he hears down the hall?

Ha! No, it is not,

but who knows what trouble these guys might be into?

The chatter is not on the roof...

no, it is coming from that new guy, John's office.

As the tired old mouse peeks through

the door, he finds Hugo, Curt, Mark,

and John around the computer...

shopping for last-minute gifts while avoiding the mall!

Close to the end of his Christmas Eve tour,
tiny JW sees Shirley... Maybin, that is!
Shirley has been to each room of
the Chapin Church campus...
to pray for its function and for every
person, young and old, who calls Chapin
Church their special church home!

"What's this?" John Wesley exclaims.
He runs in the door of room 206 from the hall.
Oh, what could it be?
Why, it is Nancy, Lisa, Mary Ann, and Lennie...

A last-minute practice.
They each want the music to reach
up to perfection, you see!

John Wesley Church Mouse VI has made all his rounds.
His old arthritic knee has been hurting
for the last thirty minutes.
But his work is important...
assigned to him long years ago by his father, the
Fifth, and his father's father, the Fourth, before that!

Oh my! How could he forget the smiling
ambassador for the church!
Who could that be?
None other than our hard-working A+ #1 custodian,
Miss Judy, with that beautiful smile on her face!
She is following behind John Wesley to see
that every bathroom, Sunday school room, and
the beautiful sanctuary all dressed up in God's
Christmas flowers are clean and ready for the
whole amazing combined congregations!

The sun is retreating below the horizon.

It soon will be time for the Christmas Eve service.

But John Wesley Church Mouse VI

has one last responsibility...a long family tradition.

This one JW cherishes greatly.

He scurries across to the big sanctuary...

where he pauses outside to look up at the cross!

No one is here yet, not even Pastor Jody.

Now John Wesley Church Mouse VI slows down

and tiptoes quietly into the dark sanctuary.

With quite a lot of struggling, because JW

is getting quite old in mouse years...

This tiny old mouse so filled with God's purpose

climbs up to the altar rail, and on tiny bent knees.

He raises his eyes to God the Father, his Creator;

Jesus the Son; and the Holy Spirit, God with

us, as old John Wesley Church Mouse VI with

a worshipful heart lifts up fervent prayers for

the Chapin Church family and all of mankind!

This story I have told is important to hear.

John Wesley III asked me to tell it so many years ago

when we met quite by accident in the little brick church

back on the other side of the road...1975 was the year!

The story will go on as long as there is a

John Wesley Church Mouse family tree!

But the main reason I tell you this story of John

Wesley and Chapin Church is this lesson to learn—

God needs us each one to be his hands and his feet!

And John Wesley Church Mouse

will tell you right quick—

God uses all sizes and all talents to be the doers

of his Word, not just pew sitters, you see!

So watch out for John Wesley Church Mouse VII.

He will be coming onboard January 1!

He will be kinda new on the job,

and you just may be lucky,

no, blessed, just like me...

to meet JW the Seventh in the halls of our church.

He will be doing God's work because
God's vision is his mission!
It is plain to see!

Now from John Wesley Church Mouse and
God's Chapin Church, filled with Jesus's love
and God's most exquisite heavenly light,
we pray you receive God's blessings and grace, along
with Jesus Christ, our Savior's most precious love…
And as church bells everywhere…ring out
all over this earth. "Joy to the World!"
A very Merry Christmas to all and
to all a blessed night!

By Evelyn Anne Johnson-Neal with John
Wesley Church Mouse. Amen!
(December 11, 2015)

John Wesley Church Mouse

1889–2020

131 years of faithful service

to God the Father, Our Creator,

Jesus Christ the Son, our Savior,

and

the Holy Spirit, God with us!

By Evelyn Anne Johnson-Neal

along with John Wesley Church Mouse

(December 12, 2015)

ABOUT THE AUTHOR

Evelyn Anne Johnson-Neal was born in North Augusta, South Carolina, right at the end of World War II. She is a Southern girl who loves the history  of the South, especially the Low Country of our southern Atlantic coastline. She is a lifelong Methodist, hence her acquaintance with John Wesley Church Mouse. She met JW by chance in the hall of the little brick church across the road from the present Chapin United Methodist Church in 1975. John Wesley asked her to write the story of the love and faith of his family and how they have watched over the ministers and staff of this growing church through a fire, a tornado, two world wars, as well as other national conflicts. Through it all, the Church Mouse family remained loyal and obedient to God and faithful to their purpose.

CPSIA information can be obtained
at www.ICGtesting.com
Printed in the USA
LVHW070124230621
690928LV00015B/1206

9 781098 035129